Heart's Planet

Shilpa Dhar

Hearts Planet

Shilpa Dhar

First
Step
Publishing
Paving Ways For New Writers

First Published in 2018 by First Step Publishing

Editorial / Sales / Marketing Office at
303-304 Garnet Nirmal Lifestyles Ph 2
Behind Nirmal Lifestyles Mall
LBS Marg Mulund West
Mumbai 400080
E-Mail:- info@firststepcorp.com
www.firststepcorp.com

ISBN:- 978-93-83306-47-3
Cover Designed by: Design Fishing
Price: INR 145 Rest $8

Chapters

Introduction

It was February and the ultimate happenings down my memory lanes were experienced in this month. Even after fifteen years of my existence on this earth, my habit of gazing at stars did not discontinue, as it had become an ingredient of my very being. As a matter of fact, I never thought it to be a sign of immaturity or childishness, as my younger brother used to call it. Almost everything in my life included them; be it, studies, sports, reading and even prayers!

As the moonbeams gave way to the piercing sunrays to acclaim another of those pleasant February days, I woke up just to feel the absence of the jewelled space embedded with dotted stars, only to make me realize how much I miss my native soil. Something peculiar about missing it was that I was no more with it. This single thought made those tears come out in an inexorable fashion as though I wanted to get rid of this pain forever. And like every other day my morning began with an inspirational note that I had sworn on my way back from the valley. Yes, it was my birthplace, the lap of my only hometown....

Tightening my black hair in a pony I dusted off my diary to invoke the memories and lessons life had offered me in a divine manner as for me;

"Life took years to preach myself;
Life took years to reach myself,
But every time I hold it i lose it the other
moment with the flow of the ink on the
paper..."

Dear diary,
Was anxious to write and am happy I found you. Today I discovered a new vista of my life.

23 July 2003
"Cutting through the various stages of this life one appears to reach a destined destiny.

Driving down to the bottom of your own self, through the various pros and cons of a situation is what makes you realize your ultimate destiny. Life was not something to be awaited as far as I was concerned. For me, it was to be realized. And my realization of self-lay just before me on my way to the valley. I took my seat alongside the window to feel the breeze full dawn. On my way up hills and down hills, I continued staring at the *Shivalik* ranges. All of them seemed to be asking a question, "if you dream of climbing the peaks of success then aren't we the destiny you are looking forward in life"? I drove past without an answer. In my life, I did the same to the achievement of any success.

On touching the feel of blissful alpine vegetation somewhere near *"Patnitop"* I could well imagine my need for a lower area, full of sufficient air to breathe, rather than the suffocating peaks of success. Success or achievement lacks a freshness to be inhaled and your arms to be exhaled, as it squeezes you to the highest degree of self-confinement. With this thought, I went forward.

I went through the rivers, up the mountains; with the deforested area and the shepherd with their livestock, all this seemed to be hectic but there was something that cried. It was life, it was a song, it was music, and something somewhere was entrapped in nature. But what was it?

Being a part of nature as I often call myself, I expected it to lie perhaps inside me too.

The sky was mourning the mountains thirsty and my feeling of being despondent was obvious felt as if I have left behind the asset of success and moved on to the woeful depth of self.

Finally, the mountain paved my way to Banihal. It was full of city shouts and life of people seemed satisfied as if nature had come to its end. The ACHIEVEMENT was there. The doubts had vanished; the smiles were back, all because there was a sense of homogeneity, a feeling of preserved culture. Small homes, women with faren and much more; the fragrance of river and the oneness of each and every drop of soil, as if it was the ultimate.

But self-saw itself broadening rather than sinking for it knew far ahead is its real-destination.

As I further drove I anticipated my destiny to be the one I left behind or perhaps the most exciting one. I had no better words to describe nature as my ecstasy of self-had killed my eagerness to speak. Without a word, I drove inside the cold Jawahar tunnel and kept my eyes fixed for the light to come my way. It was not until I crossed the tunnel that I witnessed a change. Perhaps what made me feel the difference was not only the breeze but together with it my first step to the valley.

Down my path lay the patches of paddy fields enveloped by the welcoming dusk.

But, inside me in my dilemma; itself laid a heavy soulful depth. I felt my heart weeping and its tears were not to be swallowed but to be shared, not to fall, but to be wiped, not to be shown but to be seen. And as my heart was weeping my eyes were fixed, as if just about to be driven by the astounding unearthed treasure of life. I could however not scrutinize my feelings as to know whether I was glad or sad, this mixture was in itself the understanding if my real destination in life. I understood that destiny is not made or already

11

made but it's your path, your way to your destination.

And if you are utterly conscious of your wants, your destination will make you reap that as long as you are engrossed in paving your way through your destiny.

I want to be that fearless, eagle,
To guard you from above,
I want to be the moving breeze,
And embrace you…oh! My paddy fields.

This is all that I want to do for you …MY KASHMIR….

I wept as I started coming out of my shock. None other than nature realized my notion and it wanted to weep with me. And the trees shook themselves, to silently whisper in my ear,

'Make your heart a little light
So that it may fly like an eagle up the sky;
make your soul so cosy and warm so that in its depth the entire Kashmir can fall.'

Up came a cloud from somewhere and saluted me with its rainbow shine.

And my heart knew its true destination was the sky.

And I felt like touching it as I opened up my arms to feel the happiness around and how glad; oh! How very happy was I to have realized that HAPPINESS is that what speaks and it is in being happy that we sometimes weep?

MY DESTINY WAS LIFE AND MY DESTINATION WAS ME MYSELF; THAT TODAY WAS ACHIEVED….."

Staristara…

Yes, it was Kashmir. I was talking about…

As it's very mentioned… made those hands fold for my prayers, making my belief in almighty strong enough for the anticipation of miracles to come my way anytime and this is what happened in the pages to come… quite expected ….out the latent faith I had.

As they say..........

> If GODs would appear then
> Humans would disappear
> If consciousness was awake
> Mistakes would prove fake,
> But
> If life was exposed to those
> MORTALS with less faith in GOD
> Then the name itself would cease

With this thought, 1 got ready for my next job. My eyes closed as I genuflected, deeply engrossed in my morning prayers, I was requesting for Lord's blessings to be bestowed on me and as usual, felt the copious morning rays embrace me with their divine warmth, only to feel my fragile body relaxing under God's blessings. I was praying for it to be a special day without any fret.

My few seconds of devotion were followed by an immediate and spontaneous healthy flow of contentment in a similar code of conduct like all other mornings... without having even a morsel of notion about a marvel coming down my path... carrying yet another experience...

'I seek no reason for a fruit to fall;
Unless it be for the gravity outside.
I seek no reason for life's fall,
Seek for it'
'Stop Seeking & U Stop
Weeping'…
I started humming this famous song as I was
back to my spirits…

Chapter One

Suddenly, I felt my whole body under pressure. A feeling that something heavy had pounced on it and my shoulders felt more overburdened than before. I opened my eyes, but found everything at its place, prim and properly kept as before and nothing lay over me too. Nevertheless, my hands sensed a burning sensation. I looked and gasped for the breath I missed, upon witnessing my hand's quiver, with some divine force. I shook my hands vigorously and felt something heavy drop out of my palms and over the floor onto the sheet paper. I bent and observed the paper awaiting yet another discovery to take my breath away and my anticipation of something peculiar happening was soon justified as I felt my eyeballs coming out of my eyes in curiosity and bewilderment of witnessing the paper sheet moving on its own!!!!!

My recent bolt from the blue left me chewing over the entire incident for the next few seconds. It was not until I regained my lost effectiveness that I gently moved my hand over it, only to undergo a mild irritating sensation while in touch with the astounding paper.

Being a science apprentice, I often used to visit the research laboratories for the analysis of the data I had so far gathered, "GATHERED HAY IN A SHEPHERD'S LIVESTOCK". As goes my dear brother's words for it.

I took this one along as I darted towards the lab, under the swathe of warm weather and bated breath. Upon reaching there, I went straight to the microscope that stood at one corner of the room, giving me a stare with its two adjusting screws.

"What was this happening since morning with me? All the things were beyond my own imagination and comprehension I said reflecting back to the question I had posed to myself as I put some safranin stain on the slide after having slightly tilted the paper over it to witness a drop of stain going up as probably something had dropped inside it and onto the slide. Without further delay, I set to work and kept the slide under the high power of the microscope. A feeling of dread encircled me as

I bent towards the eyepiece. I could scrutinize the movements of exhalation and inhalation of the baffling unimaginative substance. I looked up to cleanse the moistened lens in order to authenticate my recent discovery...

It was indeed a scary experience when even after doing so I analysed the same inference repeatedly.

I soon became conscious of my aloofness in the huge room without a single other human soul and the fact of the night growing nearer, so I dashed towards my home. Moreover, as far as the lens was concerned it was kept safely in a closed glass jar inside the attic room, accompanying the other data.

Exhausted with the day's work, I ended up snoring inside the cosy bed...

Chapter Two

The Mystery Prevails ... So Keep Reading

"Staristara, Staristara... wake up. It is nine already'. A guttural sound, coming from somewhere very close to my ear made me jump like an acrobat.

It was my brother. His very looks didn't take long for my frowning appearance to overshadow my sleepy features accompanying, of course, a usual puckered brow.

"You little Santa in disguise, couldn't you see I was sleeping. What was the need of bursting in my ears?" It was no use shouting, as he had left even before the sound waves would ever reach him.

Taking a glimpse at the sight of the recent crack of the dawn, I woke up with a sense of fulfilment in not remembering my ever-boring dreams.

I wanted to get back to my studies as my exams of matriculation were round the corner and I had a terrible sense of fear of not being able to score well.

This had been a reason for my many sleepless nights…and that one thought my dad narrated me throughout was like an unforgettable preaching. For him…

"Career was a parcel
That mailed us in life
But
Decisions were a key to drive our life"
And I always wondered what decisions would I be ever taking that would drive my life? And would they be that important to drive other lives as well???

And believe me, once I say this though; this question hadn't given me the smallest clue about the series of decisions that I would take… in just a matter of days".

Suddenly, I heard a scream and dashed, only to discover my tiny little brother dancing on his toes, unable to stand the recent bombshell from the crush of a jar.

It had caused a great havoc in the room filled with old peculiar objects.

"LET ME SEE", I said as I looked towards the floor. "WHAT IS SO TERRIFYING AS TO MAKE MY LITTLE BROTHER RUN OFF HIS FEET"? I exclaimed with a sweet chuckle.

"Just A broken empty glass jar" yelled my brother without further delay. That is no more an empty one, I thought as the whole scene of the day before recapitulated in my brain, only to make me shiver from top to bottom.

Well, that's it BUT wait a minute! Where could that tiny little thing be??

But before searching for it I never did once forget the horrific scene of the blood dripping from my brother's ankle after having stepped over it and snooped to have a look at it. "Why did you ever run post haste so as to make the poor jar jump of its place? Bad boy, now looks here I am not expecting the same from you again." I said after half gulping down my saliva of anxiety, overpowered with an unknown fear of not having known as how to discriminate the sudden outbreak a few seconds before.

But his reaction made my ears stand out, as he denied it to be an accident caused by him, a fact hard to be overlooked, was one with the mention of ....

'I just happened to be, passing when I heard the crash!!!!' And the baseball went up and down the floor following a trail of terror down my spine. It was yet another event, to be memorized by me for further speculations on a few conclusions.

"Was it just a guess??...
Creating such a mess.......
Or a star
Shining far afar..........
Perhaps a never solved mystery,
Covering a long moor in the coming history."
I hummed

"Left for u to solve, Staristara, a *mysterstara* like the countless stars," he said half teasing as we both caught a glimpse of a shining star far far miles apart.

However, it wasn't before I remembered having dropped myself out of this perplexing situation that I slept in peace...

Chapter Three

Live Up For The Thrill

With a yawn perhaps the last one for the day, I stepped out quite relaxed with my ample dose of the night. Get ready to live up for the shock was a quick message to my own self as I braced up for embracing each and every second of the much-awaited day.

It was a different day, with a lull of achievement shining brightly through the sky, accompanied with optimism floating in the cloudy air.

My observation changed my opinion and my positive imagination clouded my earlier one. Stepping out of my suspicious thoughts, I finally landed in the garden. "Gosh!! A TOMATO......"

I exclaimed quite surprisingly as it happened to come within my vision. I never knew we had those squeaky little things in our lawn. With a slight bend towards it, I was stuck.

Stuck to clear my thought as it consistently blamed my sight, blamed me for I knew what I saw a second or so ago. Moving a little closer I knew it. I knew it was moving.... With bends and curves, up on my leg and wait a minute, it's on my head... oops on my hands.

It had two eyes, one nose, and,... a it kissed me a second ago, with those blood red lips...and smiled as though it had never known how too. With all his strength he went laughing that tickled my hands and made me giggle.

"Who are you???"
I said filled with excitement at my recent so-called exceptional jackpot or it is what I call it or felt it.

"I am a heart...."
It spoke with a voice like any other gentleman would have had.

Indeed it was, I saw it, as though it had increased in its size.

It was expanding; soon there laid a big big heart before me.

A heart that spoke. That laughed.

It was happening too fast. Faster than an apple fall and perhaps faster than the time Newton took in realizing its cause.

"I know what's in your mind," he said, "but I am neither Newton nor his apple."

I have a history, a small one though....

"Staristara,,, Staristara   hey what are u doing there."

"That's my mom and bro come I will take you in and hide you."

I said, here we go faster than wind lighter than air...

up the stairs in the room and here you go in the big jar, with abundant holes on its lid, to let u live.

We were laughing away when my bro Gopsi entered. I quickly hid it beneath my pillow. IT DIDN'T take him long to realize that I was hiding, a so-called known mystery. A mystery that taught me how to observe... Is what I still remark about it.

"Will you be my friend? ". A voice, from beneath my pillow made my bro

Soar up in the air or it was what I imagined him to be doing."
G........GH..........GHO...GHO................... ghost!!! GHOST..............................."

SCREACHED GOPSI.

"He is a mystery." Was my only, probably unsatisfied, small response to his long exclamation

"A mystery."
Is all he could say assembling his bits of breath back into himself. "What kind of a mystery sis. The one with voices and no physical appearance, no figure............ and what about the voice a few minutes back. Who wants us to be his friends? Do you know something about it? Please tell me about him" he said in one breath.

"He is a heart. He is life. And life is a friend. So, he is our friend."

So saying I pulled out a calm looking face outside, quite gently from beneath my pillow. And from that October, morning three of us were friends... FRIENDS FOR A LIFETIME

Chapter Four

The Adventure Begins

Like every morning in this one week that passed Hearty, what I named my heart friend as woke me up and we went for walk. Of course, he used to be safely hiding in my waistcoat pocket. Quite safely kept he used to be away from the mean eyes of this world.

From the mean eyes of the world, I mean only my world and not Hearty's. He had a different world and today he expressed it all. All that he had in his history; all that brought him here, and all that I wrote in my diary today night in my bed.

28 Oct,
Dear Pal, "THE DIARY",

LOVE is all what I learned today; every breath of mine was washed with the sweet essence of love that whirled within my soul, in a way that it healed a lot of misassumptions about GOODNESS. Yes, it exists, it truly does. My spirit was awakened on knowing where hearty belongs; it's a place, very far from here. It's the **"HEARTS PLANET"**. A planet where hearts like hearty live.

The obvious answer, as Hearty declared it to be, concerning the crush of the jar, in the attic room many nights back, was conveyed by him to me in a manner that made me have faith in science to an extent that I wanted to meet other hearts like Hearty, also to a level that never came down for the rest of my life in believing more than knowing that hearts do have a value. A value whose base rests on EMOTIONS...

He surprisingly survived on emotions. He ate emotions. When I found myself gay he would expand as if this is what he had been waiting for all through, like a person who would depend on food for LIFE...

And that one incident in the lab made me realize that life is similar to an experiment.

'Its (life) one such experiment
In which without performing one,
Life is examined.'

Chapter Five

Ahead Of Life And Time

Morning found me in my diary…

And Hearty too. "Good morning, hearty" in my half sleeps state I wished Hearty. "A very big morning to you" he said. "Why in the world do you call it a big morning? "Was my direct query, on his plump red face.

"He calls it a big morning as this is what people there call him."

Gopsi said in one tone. "People where?" I asked my bro who happened to be behind me, nicely lying in a chesterfield.

"They call it a big morning as people; hearty people on the hearts planet become BIG with love and good wishes." He answered "and PESSIMISM makes them squeeze and fall down. This is what exactly took place that night. I spoke with full understanding.
"Which night" Gopsi intervened. "When you hurt your ankle, the crush of the jar took place

before you got hurt simply because of the one chief reason that I was being rude to you. Hearty must have shrunk and…"

"… The jar fell down on the floor" said hearty in a jiffy.

"Now, that everything is clear to me, let's go and party"

The other moment that I remember, we were all partying outside, in the open lawn of a restaurant. "Billiards", one of the famous in the town, famous for its pizzas. .

"What would we order for you, a pizza, or, an EMOTIONAL PIZZA" I questioned hearty for his….reply from within my jacket ……

"Anything, but food" replied hearty.

Well, he just enjoyed and the more he enjoyed the more he expanded.

Not so much, as he was safe till the morning to come.

Chapter Six

Remain In A Fix

LIFE couldn't be more exciting than the thought of making a dream come true, a dream that had behind it, doors to a real vision. A real vision called life...and I was on my journey to help it become a reality ...

"Hearty, I have a dream, will you listen," I said to hearty, still lying in my bed.

"Sure,"
"I want to meet life..."
"What kind of a life?"

"I want to see the 'HEARTS-PLANET' and not be, but perhaps feel like one. I want to feel my heart, Hearty....will you help me... go up there...." I spoke to him as if he was forty years elder to me.

Never had been my speech or the pitch in which I spoke so horrible to make someone weep, but to my shock, this time I made someone weep.

"What's the matter Hearty?

"I miss my family. I wish I had them here today. They always said earth people aren't good to good hearts. They stopped me from coming here, the reason being that I would not be able to survive, due to lack of love, and would die... but you proved it out today Stari... that True Hearts Never Die...

"And you know why, as Hope Never Dies..."

So saying we both wept to our heart's content... And Then We Filled Our Heart With Hope...and quite uneventfully braced up for the journey to come.....

Chapter Seven

Let's Go And Cross The Heaven

"Gopsi, are you coming, with me to the Hearts planet?"

As it is, mom and dad are out for a month or so, till then let's shine out up there on the sky...what do you say about it...?" Were the first few words that came out of me, early that morning, in a way so fast that I couldn't believe my speed ...?

"As you say; always at your service, but only for the trip."

As guided by Hearty we tied few wires around him and connected them with the socket of the computer.

After giving a lot of instructions, we waited patiently for an aircraft.

Finally, it arrived and once it did the other moment we all were in it, and it took up so fast that in terms of physics it may be called as" Faster Than The Vision Of Human Sight"

As beautiful as heaven, as delicate as life, as blissful as dawn...as incomprehensible as philosophy ....my thoughts completely enrobed me, about the place, on watching it, even my eyes felt in their full, hilt of sensitivity.

"Here we are, over and onto the HEARTS-PLANET," said Hearty, too excited to hide it.

"It looks as though made for the hearts...." I spoke.

"Stari, as per the custom, we are first supposed to report to the esteemed king of hearts and queen of hearts and then roam about freely on this planet."

The planet was smaller than the earth and was without any division between countries or continents.

The palace was as colourful, as a modern art painting. It had something unique in it. It was the windows that it had. Not exactly windows but the numbers in which they shone brightly on the tall walls of the castle. With quite a dozen on one face of the wall and a cute heart on each window.

"Are they there for protection purpose? "I questioned hearty out of a sudden curiosity, felt for the strange place in my HEART.

HEART, as far as my heart was concerned it was too full of gaiety as though it had found its world.

"Not at all. They are here for love" answered Hearty.

"They look so cute with those welcoming eyes."

"Indeed they do. Come let's enter the palace."

On my first step inside, my feet felt the pure essence of all variety of flowers, they with their freshness appeared quite pleasing.

"Do you have plants on your planet too?"

"Sure, we have them and they grow in the same way as we do."
The aisle was filled with flowers and the dazzling walls were all full of different colours.

It opened into a bright and big hall.

"Big morning, sockh; sockh to your majesty. I have with me a friend and her brother from earth."

All this time Gopsi was with me, but in my thoughts so happily engrossed was I that I lost the opportunity to feel his presence around me.

King of hearts wore a robe, with diamond dust on it, and had a crown studded with hearts, carved out of blue stones. Queen was oppositely peculiar. She had a crown made up of red, deep red petals. That perhaps matched with her face colour too. She was too charming to resist speaking too.

"Staristara, is that your name? "Asked the king.
"Yes, your majesty I am Staristara," I said.

"You are our guest. With full love, we welcome you to the HEARTS-PLANET.
We invite you and Gopsi with hearty to have a talk with us tomorrow morning so that we get to know each other."

With grateful smiles on our face, we left. The king had made arrangements for our stay. It was a place near the palace.

As soon as we reached there, we relaxed and then Gopsi and I had dinner, we bought with us. Finally, we all slept...but for me.

I couldn't help pondering on the various faces I saw today and the fact I was no more in the world, but far somewhere away from mom and dad and chuckled at the thought of my dad guessing me to be amidst hearts in the hearts planet.

Whatever it was, nevertheless I was enjoying each an every iota of a second there and had lost the words for expressing it

It was a heaven of my dreams...I wondered as I caught a glimpse of a thick covered book on the shelf right opposite me. It appeared as though had not been touched for decades

It had a peculiar mystic aura encircling it.
I slipped out of my bed and wore my slippers...
And encouraged me to move ahead.......................
It was of a bright red colour that shone strikingly in the night...
As I picked it up I realized it to be astonishingly bulky.
And quickly placed it safely on the table nearby.
My curiosity was at its pinnacle. "I want to go through it now." I thought and switched on the table light.

The first page was blank. I slipped my fingers on to the next page and it came before me in a beautiful italic calligraphic handwriting.

Soon I had poetry in front of me written In ancient
Black fountain ink................

The Phantom

Wearing a gown of chenille
And sitting on one of the castles pantiles
She watched the angelicas drip line
Over the hatched trial

She wore a choker
During her sojourn in the castle cell
And looked like an anemone
With an oyster in a seashell

As the cherub, took the trug
With the beauteous petunia
Of the verbena
To the beano
In the evanesce scenario…

In post-haste, she went to chase
But oh! The loam
Rick with foam

"In it was only a PANTOMIME"
She could only sigh
For a sight
Of the divine…

41

As the sky turned russet
And the sun was about to set

Her PHANTOM gleaned
To ebb
In the month of Feb.

As she pensuid
In the scene
For it to protean
In the serene eve

To embrace
The cascade
Of JOY…

"Looks like an epic…"
I thought after its completion…
"Will tell about this to Gopsi in the morning, he might find this a bit interesting as he is a fond reader of magical classics…" was my last thought in bed as I closed my eyes for a final entry in the land of magnificent dreams…

Chapter Eight

The Hearts Planet

"Let's go and play, hide and seek, Stari... please. "Screeched Gopsi in a tone that made me realize that his pitch was much softer and delicate on this planet, as it didn't take a moment for me to refuse.

"Let's go and hide," I said excitedly.

On this beautiful planet, hiding proved to be indeed exciting and joyful.

"Here I caught you, Gopsi, hiding below the broken ...."

"It's me"

"Oh! Hearty, you almost took my breath away, but if it was you, then where is Gopsi.........?"I cried.

Let's go and look out for Gopsi.

We walked past over the red dusty surface......and kept our eyes fixed on the long trail that never happened to end.

We were soon acquainted with Gopsi sitting far away on the ground.

"What are you doing here?" I asked him as we came nearer. He had before him a heart nicely seated on a big shaft made up of large log pieces and I guess that the heart was telling him something.

Hearty introduced us to that heart......Panun was her name.

"Sis, you know her tale, please sit here and listen."

So here we all were listening to the most poignant narrative ever and the listeners were I, Gopsi, and Hearty.

Chapter Nine

Hope Its Going Fine

She was a pale heart that appeared quite weak to me... but carried a strange feeling of goodness in her eyes.

'Like a perfume embraces the body, Let the foul smell to do so let the eternal bliss of your mind Mould it to a fragrance." she started.

"I believed in this philosophy of life when I was there on EARTH.

I tried to love and spread it with affection in every deed of mine. But, I was killed psychologically, brutally.

Lord, of love, sent me to this planet as consent, to my Faith, Patience and Love for him and his creations.

Right from my parents, my very part of blood, to my LOVE and even to my enemies ......my love was until the end of time equivalent for all."

'If "I" was a name

Maybe life would have been famous in fake fame

But, "I" is not a name but an aim in itself.
I achieved my aim after a great struggle on the earth, but perhaps, loss on earth was not as immense in essence.'

"To, you, I say Staristara...go ahead and serve, serve and serve.....But never weep as a divinity has made good places for good souls...

'Sometimes to pay a price
We spend money
While still another time
To pay for our debts of sins
We spend the life with the
Debt of Pain.'

'Believe in it and life on earth will be easier....'

We all stood mesmerized in her absorbing speech.

"Would you please explain a morsel of your long journey on earth?" I requested. "Sure!!!!" She answered willingly.

"I hear no music, no sound; I feel no motion in all that rests around Me." this is what I said to myself during my life on earth.

"Life lacks rhythm; a rhythm which makes a dumb; deaf or a lame feel obliged to the creator for realizing their pain. But to normal humans what I inferred he has closed all doors; for I guess; perhaps it appears; he has no feelings for; rather no time for us, were some of my thoughts pertaining to the creator."

"My FAITH was on its verge of sinking, life with goodness on its verge of ending...

When I saw the scars fading as a feeling so pure prevailed over it to encircle my doubts about the WORLD. World of mortals where life began with breaths and ends with the same and in between it, no time to know it, the world in the fast rush of our own self-centred lives."

"Goodness is dawned when the spirit is high;
Life is bestowed with treasures infinite when
TRUTH is sown"

"Was what acted as an exceptional relief at
that point in life."

Gopsi intervened at this point, to know about
TRUTH...

"TRUTH... means fact. Isn't it?"
"Truth meant life for me, obeying each and
every penalty of nature; I had to come across a
lot of misunderstandings. No, one really
understood me on earth "'I wish immortality
of acceptance would rest in the mortals.'
"Truth is not just a fact, but something that I
lived for, a purpose, a spirit; it dealt with a
friend of mine.......a source of true happiness"

"Did you lose him?" I asked

"I lost him through the hands of the world and
he soon became a part of fakeness."

"I really loved that soul a lot, even remembering, that makes the pain deeper, though now he is on the earth."

"What is he doing there?" I asked
"He is living his next life; and from above I am always praying for him."
"He is a fine soul; I wish if only he understood me"

"He believed that …something's are inside; while others outside; but something's not everything is only in this life….
But, I believed that outside there is a better world. And my belief came out to be truthful."

"Stari, always remember…"" lit are the eyes of those who live and blessed are the hands of those who give."

"We had a cool life, until one day he started realizing that he doesn't like me, probably because he was busy, busy not to know life, but to, only to be more materialistic, anyhow, since then nothing took place for good, I joined missionary services later …………although always remembered him in the eyes of a child playing by, in the warmth of a mother and in the hope, hope to see him one day."

"Did you see him?"

"Yes I did, when I was sixty-four during my last days of pilgrimage I went to see him. He didn't recognize me.... He was old... with a stick and bifocal specs. With his last glance, I passed away....."

"Was that all that you had in your being......." exclaimed I in a way that it made her smirk.

"Life wasn't easier at the service I joined too, as, at the rear of the act of lending a hand a lot of misdeeds were conducted. I fought for it single-handedly ....such was the plight of the world on the earth.....A WORLD of my DREAMS had now become a home of nightmares..."

"Overpowering your thoughts with actions is what people do...
But the domination of truth over thoughts flows in the minds of nobles."   I said after weighing up the entire situation.

"Stari, you are talking like Panun. For the first time I am feeling like being glad about you, concerning what you spoke a second ago," said Gopsi panting!

"I really mean it; I only wish God made more nobles like you," I said to Panun.

"The fact that you are here, seems to me that he has made one before me. I in person feel that youths like you, form an important branch of the human culture.....that is HUMANITY." Believed Panun.

"Panun will you be our friend?" I asked.
"Why not!"Panun replied.
"Now, let's bash up for the eve party...." shouted hearty from somewhere.
"What kind of eve-party.?" Gopsi said.

"King Of Hearts Has Planned An Exciting Eve-Party For The Guests And Also Has A Surprise During It." said, Hearty.

"So, let's meet at the party then...Bye." I said as we all moved back to our particular places, on the planet.

But I kept thinking of Panun and unknowingly started relating my pain to hers. And I knew what I was missing right now felt the same breeze pass by me, the same fragrance encircling me, the same touch calling me the same love whispering In my ears and flowing in my veins

Yes, it was the same love, the same forbidden love of my Kashmir... that had an aching feeling.
I felt a strong desire to share her pain I felt like offering her something.
And I knew what.
Soon I took a pen and wrote a woeful tale
For Panun

"QUENCH"

She watched
The midnight sea wrapped
Under the moonlight of glee
Filled with an insatiable plea
To fulfil the never-ending QUENCH
Of the reflective sea
Of the winsome midnight sea
Embedded with stars
Its beauty lay afar
For decked with waves were the glorious
moon rays
And inside its watery cover
Lay the sumptuous pearls
In and over the
Magnificent Midnight Sea
A pebble broke the midnight silence
And brought about wavy ripples

As she heard the prince on the other bank said
"Oh! The moon you look so gay, with the stars
as your crown
Still, it's the sea where you drown
And your beams touch the watery realms to
make the sea
Ever SERENE

I can't envisage a life like a cage…..
So let the moon extinguish forever
Leaving behind all the terror".

She cried but in vain
With a heartfelt pain
"The moon can't die; it can only hide behind
the dark
Clouds that lie
Over the sky,
But never can it die,
Biding the sea a goodbye

He replied, "I want to dead end my life so
dead and want to bloom in the oceany bed"

So saying;
She saw him float
In the midnight sea
And she could only pensive….
For the lost hidden glee
Lost forever in her oceany eyes
In the woeful cries
As She Was The Sea
And He The Moonlight Of Glee
That Forever Got Free

Leaving A Dark Abondand Sea Forever Life
Free"

Staristara

I folded the paper in which I delicately penned it down and rolled it to place it gently beside my cushion.

Nevertheless couldn't sleep in peace as the thought of Panun continuously triggered in my mind.

Chapter Ten

With My Pen

Our first step that eve landed us in the most striking, benevolent and inconceivable terra firma of the king of hearts.

What made it breath-taking was the hearts dancing, all around in a welcoming manner. With beams all over, we were left awestruck to believe what our eyes discovered a moment prior to now.
"Hi," a voice from back whispered in my ear.
"Oh! Hi, Panun. We all were waiting for you." said Hearty, pleasantly.

"You are looking splendidly cool, Panun," I told her.

"I am starving, let's enter." sniveled Gopsi.

In next to no time, we all were in the castle, enjoying the feast we had. Gopsi and I only had the meal, rest were reliant only on dances and other pleasure-giving items performed by various hearts.

"I have a surprise this eve for the most beautiful, heart out here." the queen of hearts spoke, with an overwhelming accent.

"Please, with a round of applause, greeted with a standing ovation, the most eternal couple of the time. Not a single but two of them together. As I say 'names are lost in the winds of life, but eternity is preserved in the bosom of strives'. Further added the king of hearts.

With all eyes fixed, a glow of radiance came upon every face, as the beams of light, from the projector, spread on to Panun and the other unfamiliar new heart.

"She has got her lost love, he was sent to this planet, after spending a different life on earth, a life of a saint." declared the king of hearts.

"PANUN AND MYON" shouted Hearty.

The next split second, we found both of them on the stage.

Too euphoric to hide it, both of them enrobed in one single beam of light, appeared as if made for each other, on the planet of jubilant manifestation, on a planet that not only gave me an idea about what love, in depth is but together with it how to spread it. People say life is all given and take, but I feel it's all regarding "give and get".

"This is my appeal to Myon, to verbalize with all of us so that we get to know each other", requested the queen of hearts in an exceptionally well-bred approach.

"I want to swim in the depths of eternity,
And want to fly through the horizon of
ambiguity,
Something somewhere stops me,
Awaking call to the other world,
Galloping the joys of this world,
Bidding farewell to the last tribute, of the
whistling kites,
Making my way through the cascades light,
I want to drop myself in the bosom of another
life,
With joys infinite,
The birds flying to embrace me,
The trees brimming to trace me,
Oh! Life this is eternal,
Surely immortal are its ways of creation and
re-creation,
From life to life,
From birth to rebirth,
From sunset to sunrise,
From dusk to dawn,
I am born, again reborn……."

Recited Myon.

"This is how I used to feel on earth, completely suffocated in my next life, but I knew that someone, somewhere is waiting for me and now I have come back to that good soul." Spoke Myon.

"May you be remembered through the passing time?
And may your remembrance defeat the time in its race of permanent
Memory." Quoted the queen of hearts. As the auditorium was filled with hips
And hoorays. , on hearing the thoughts of Myon.

"Panun, would you say a bit of what you are feeling current." Solicited Myon.

"I don't know what to say oh! I don't believe it love you God!"

"My questions are confined to my tears,
My answers to my dilemma,

This is all that I am, rest lacks words." Sobbed Panun.

On hearts planet, every miracle is possible, I thought.

After the disclosure was over, Panun and Myon went personally, to meet everyone at the party.

"These are my friends, Staristara, Gopsi, and Hearty. "Introduced Panun to Myon. "Jovial, to meet you, "said Myon.

"Same here." We all replied in one tone.

Having a great party we all felt heavy-eyed. "I think we all must go home now and put our feet up so that tomorrow senses happiness on seeing us. GOOD NIGHT. "The king of hearts announced in between.

So we all concluded our talks for a night-time gap.

Chapter Eleven

More.... To It...

"Truth and time, steal the past,
To perceive the future,
Steal the failure,
To perceive the victory,
BADE THE MORTAL....,
TO ETERNITY......."

This is what I inferred, from the classic episode of and about LIFE, a day back on the hearts planet.

As per the kings' proclamation, the morning saw me in a great and awe-inspiring frame of intellect, as was palpable, from the sudden change in my behavioural pattern that Monday morning.

"Gopsi, would you take the trouble of waking up." I stated.

"Lets, go and catch up with others......."Gopsi to a certain extent sounded perfectly right as 'once gone can never be caught....'

We got prepared, and instantly reached the castle to meet the king and the queen of hearts.

"A big, morning to your majesty."I said on entering the foyer.

"Morning, morning, Stari.....we were waiting for you, we had an issue to thrash out with you. "King of hearts reacted sparingly.

"At your service, sir. Please, do tell me what I can do for you?" I said.

"Last night, we took notice of what was spoken by Panun in your context. I got the information that you are an exceptionally sensitive, talented adolescent who has ahead of her assorted directions, in which she can do plenty, with a ready to serve nature, so we thereby request you to be, of some use in getting rid of the impurity present in the world-I mean on the EARTH. "Spoke the king.

"I will try my best sir." I said at the thought that how much do they think about our earth, and the inhabitants there don't have a point in time to even think so.

"Sir, a few nights back I read a poem from a book that lay on the shelf and found it typical of a legendry expression. Can you tell me it belongs to whom?"

"Oh! Stari. I remember that is an attic written by my grandfather's daddy's daddy. You know, I mean great great great grandfather. I mean the greatest of them all. The oldest, the one who was the first on this planet," said the king.

"Why? Stari, u can always have it if u like it."
"Thank-you so much would love to have it"......I soon replied excitedly.

After this we left, and geared up for the last day on the planet that was to come after a short, yet long span of twenty four hours. It was short as I had to do many things in one day, and extensive, as , somewhere down us were waiting to return home.

23rd of February, invited all the hearts to gather in the king of hearts antechamber, a big one.

"Please be seated, today we all have assembled here to give our unsurpassed, good wishes to Staristara and Gopsi, for their future life to come. We do also, wish, they become a part like us in their heart, be sincere to their own hearts, so that at the right time we can live together with them at the same planet –OUR VERY OWN HEARTS PLANET. Three cheers to it. Hip-hip-hooray, hip-hip-hooray, hip-hip-hooooooooray!!!

Stari we order you to make our size big, by an emotional speech." king of hearts said irrepressibly giggling.

And the next thing that I remember, I was on the stage, weeping out my state of mind.

"I am a very small person. I don't own much. But whatever little I have, however, small it may be, I will feel it my greatest pleasure to share it with you all here. And do believe me, when I say, you are worth more, and I do wish

I had more, to give more. Every little gesture of yours will always be remembered by me in a way that I will always spread them, selflessly. You all taught me that

'Life is not to give,
But to spread,
It is not to feel,
But to let it feel,
It is not to speak,
But to let it speak,
It is not to live,
But to be alive for others,

That we do in living......for true life...'
I will be on earth for service. Since, the very day I met Hearty, life took a change and that small change, gave me a garland of a different, good philosophies about life. Panun and Myon were equally great in enlightening me about, love. Faith, Friend, and Goodness, mere few letter words, proved to be a key to the cosmic treasure of wisdom.
If only everyone on earth had a chance to feel so."

Gopsi added, "I don't know really what to say. But if truth be told, I'll be indeed missing you all. bye, and have lots of emotions."

After a grand celebration of the farewell, we were all set to leave...

Chapter Twelve

In The End

We left the planet, with all good wishes surrounding us, with we, I mean just Gopsi and me.

We returned, in the same mode as we had left. Mom and dad were to return in the evening. Gopsi, worn-out went directly in the bed and I was left, writing, with a pen in my hand. I wrote it all, all I had experienced. And all I had learnt.

Chapter Thirteen

A Final Task Of My Teens

"Hey, Staristara.................
Look what's the headline today" shouted
Gopsi ....

"Yes, tell my Golu, what has happened in this
world that has made me. Bro so excited early
in the morning." I said kissing him gently on
his forehead.

He handed me "The Tribune", one of the
famous newspapers of the town.

*"Thousands Of Innocent Lives Killed As Plane
Crashes Into World Trade Center By Terrorists."*
I read out loud.

"I can't believe it, Gopsi. This is heights.
Heights of pain. I mean look at this. Just look at
this. All happening in this world. in my world.
In our world gopsi. This is so sinful."

"I know, sis. but what can we do??

Except look at the paper for a news every morning. probably expecting such news time and again......" said Gopsi soulfully.

"No, we have to do something. After all, we had promised the king of hearts and we can't run away from our promises."

"Hey, the phones ringing check out who is there Gopsi..."

"Hello"

"Ya, sure I have done all the homework. You can have my register of solved sums."
"Ya, bye....."
"Who's it Gopsi?"
"A class fellow calling up for work".
"Is coming in the evening.."
"Ok"
The day passed on quickly, though we had little to perform and accomplish.
At 4pm the doorbell rang.
"Gopsi, it must be your Friend, please open the door. I bolted it a few minutes back".
"Hey .....Shaukat....."

"How you doing ...long time...I have kept the register for you. First, have a cup of tea with us..."

"Ya sure.." He replied as he introduced his sister, Shabana to us....who had accompanied him.

"Hye, Shabana how you doing." I am Staristara."

"Pleased to meet you"

And then as time flew we started discussing nothing but each other.

"We both belong to Paristhan...but currently my dad is posted here", Shabana said.

"We too do.....and our fate posted us here. I was hardly three when our house was burnt in the valley and we lost faith in humanity. I had made lots of friend's there and lost them all as we migrated. We used to play with snowballs, celebrate Diwali and Eid together. ...but then all became victims of hatred for each other."

"Where did you belong to in Kashmir"?
"Well, I was from, downtown, in Paristan"

71

"What did you say? Kanth Paristan? I mean..remember me. I am the girl, Shabana......and you are the same Stari, stargazer...what a miracle...? Never thought we would be meeting this way."

Then there was a silence of few minutes, as I felt like hugging her but there was something that was missing.....perhaps, the same old love for each other was still the same but had lost its expression with the flow of destiny.....

"Oh! Shabana, though I am the same, our pains and paths are different now. You can never relate to my feelings now..."

"I can Stari. I know what you and other Paristani Pandits Have gone through."
"I can help you..."She answered bluntly.
"But we have lost confidence in YOU,"I said coldly.
"But we have confidence in you."
And I will prove you this by letting you know a secret......
A secret, that no one is aware of.
"What kind of a Secret?"

So saying she silently slipped her hand in mine and moved me to the adjoining room. After bolting the door room inside, she said it all. All that could have been a turning point in any relationship that ever was in this world. A turning point or probably the end of the most delicate bond between a brother and his sister. Between Shabana and her brother.

Stari my elder brother is the head of a prominent terrorist organization. I will take you to him. You can tell him the pain of separation that you have gone through and record the conversation.

"Ya.....but"
"No, but .....And all. I have a strong hunch that your passion for Paristan will make him a better person. Will you help me?
"Ok"
"Gopsi, get ready, tomorrow early in the morning.............we are going to Paristan and facing what's store for us."
I said in one breath.............................

"Okay" winked Gopsi at the thought of yet another adventure coming our way.

After a day of pensive mood, Gopsi from nowhere came running and shouted.
"Hey, sister. Just take a chill pill. Look what do I have for you? I am proud of you."

He said handing me a paper on which he had something in store for me

Mystery Of A Hand

One hand to tell you
Your future
One hand to reap your
Lives treasure
But apart from this, it hath some feelings too
When you pick a child
In your arms and you hold a delicate gift
In your palms
With a feeling of tenderness
Never found
Carrying a deep sensitive bound
When you hug a life
And you wipe a tear which moistens your
hand
And makes you swear
A promise for a near or dear
But.....its

Only then when you join them together
You really pray

Forgetting that hidden somewhere
In your very own hands
Lies a truthful magic wand
Not on your palmic lines
But in your actions so divine……..

Gopsi…..
"Thanks, Gopsi. That's lovely on your part"

"We have to help our world. And we will no matter what the fate."

Early the next morning at four, we braced for the travel.

We took a plane for Paristan with Shabana, that was half an hour from our place.

"Look at the snow-clad glaciers, down"
"Ya, they are simply awesome" I replied to Gopsi.
"Well here's something for them, written in the magazine, look!"

In Memory Of A Glacier

In the marmoreal glaciers of nature
I kneel
To unveil
My heart's fountains

There is a full verity
In every serenity
Of nature's marmoreal glaciers.....

It ambles down
With the icy crown
To acclaim suns rays
Filled with praise
For the glaciers magnificent gaze

It shows no regret
To avow its secret
And melts in solicitude
Which indeed is verisimilitude
Amidst all the feeble
It appears amiable

For it is the sun it idolizes
And rises
To purify its glory

In veritable
Memory
Of THE GLACIER IT ONCE WAS....!!!!!!!!!!"

"That's a good one."
"Ya, you are right provided someone understands it........." laughed Gopsi........................

I burst into laughter at his spontaneous answer.

After having landed in Paristan we moved towards an unknown place....in a closed jeep that had come to the airport to receive us.
Once the jeep stopped we all moved out and followed Shabana blindly, hardly aware about the place. All I could know was from the surrounding that we were on the top of some kind of a huge hill, with tall trees surrounding us.

Finally, we entered a small hut. It was dark from the inside.

Soon a tall person, the head of all terrorist organizations placed himself on one of the chairs on the stage right in front of us. He was hugely built and had a long beard.

"Looks like he will wipe the floor with his beard" chuckled Gopsi.

"Shh…" I said.
Soon we were introduced by Shabana to him.
"Excuse me" declared Gopsi loudly in his full spirits.
"Not now Gopsi"
"It's now or never" I had never seen Gopsi in such an anger.
"Yes…" he replied.

"When I play hockey in school, I play it with the person who has a stick with him and knows the rules. Tell me a single hockey champion who played with the spectators………..
Or name any cricket player who handed the ball in the audience or simply kept on striking the ball at the audience with his bat……….

Your fight for Kashmir is with the innocent people of the country or with the administration.

You are targeting the people just like targeting the audience who are hardly aware of the norms and rules of the game.

Of the game that you are playing on the hundreds and millions of people picking up chunks of peace from their lives.

It's like involving a cat in the game of two monkeys.

I won't ask for the solution of my math's problem nor would I hit you for not knowing the answer, then why do you?

Can you answer me???
 Can you answer this to a ten-year-old child?

I want to tell you, sir, that your son too is of my age.

Would you like to see his fate swinging in the hands of two countries or two people?
Let's decide it once and for all. LET THE GAME END.

He had spoilt everything I thought. We weren't turning back home I thought. Even Shabana was in a state of shock and utter disbelief.....

So saying he went near him and stood right opposite him, without anyone even uttering a single word. I wonder if such a silence would have ever existed in this universe.

The next thing what Gopsi did was unbelievable.
As if his white full sleeves shirt and dark blue jeans were the last ones he was wearing.

A strange quiver passed onto me. And I felt the darkness encircle me...no sooner I realized I was fainting into an unknown world without any guesses...

Chapter Fourteen

"No please we don't want any publicity. Please keep off the door. Let them wait …." The voice fainted gradually, not that I had again fainted but the ….voice was moving away…..

The walls were sparkling white in colour without a single stain to bother my eyes. There was a sleekly fitted air conditioner in the wall right opposite to me. Blue coloured silken curtains were providing a fabulous cover to the glass windows.

On my right lay a wooden table and wait a sec!!!

On it was a huge bouquet of red rosebuds…with jasmine stalks that filled the room with fragrance and made their presence felt.

"Hey, sis. Hope you well or should I call the doctors?" It was Gopsi speaking out the moment he came in.

Am I in a hospital?
"Ya, in an A grade hospital…with all the luxuries, AC, Jacuzzi……

"Wait please wait…..
What's wrong with you?
I mean what's wrong with me…I mean. I know I fainted. But what am I doing here?
I mean in a five-star hospital?"

"Look, sis, I know you want to know it all. All that happened last evening….
"You ok Gopsi. You took my breath away. Why in the world did you do that?"

"Well switch on any news channel and look for yourself" he chuckled.

And as he switched on the screen television on the wall I could see it all and I smelt it all, as I understood what actually happened.

"Here's your gun and here is me. Shoot me if you think I am wrong. Let my life lie in your hand…..
Let's see who wins.

My belief that you are wrong or my gun?

But before doing that sir I've a request…

Imagine that your son is at my place, forgetting that I am an INDIAN." so saying Gopsi closed his eyelids in a divine style.
"And there's where I fainted."
"I AM SORRY"

Was the heads reply and all the continents could view those tears in his eyes as he fell on his knees and surrendered in that small hut and the recorded conversation was being telecasted time and again.
A history was created.
And soon I realized we were as well on camera.
As I found a journalist comes with a camera in our room.
I could see myself live.
"How did you and Gopsi make it possible?" asked Deepak from KDTV.

We had a promise with ourselves, with this world and with each other. This is what made it possible. A single Promise. A single commitment to be responsible for what goes wrong with ourselves and with our country and with the world and yes without the help of Shabana it would still have been a dream.....

The bouquet, on the right of me, was from her. She proved it that friends are above religion.

"And little champion what made you put your life at a stake?"
"Everything Is Gained And Perhaps Faces A Loss
Gain Yourself So That The Fear Of Losing Is Gone Forever"
And I gained myself by putting my life at stake.

Late that night I thought
"If likings were admirable;
I would have liked to admire"
"If beauty was appreciable, I would have never let it down;
But if LIFE was as delicate as beauty and likings I would stand
Stiff to guard it and would have ignored the rest"

This is what Gopsi did. He stood stiffly to guard so many lives. I am PROUD OF HIM. I THOUGHT TO MYSELF......

As I Caught A Glimpse Of An Article Written By A Handicap For The Terrorist Activity Groups.
In His Small Little Way To Contribute To This Society

"In The Voice Of A Handicap"

Do I crave?
Inside my lively grave.
Then why do you?
Oh! People if should you yell;
Before you must tell;
Why are you making this earth a hell?
Two hands to work and serve the world;
Still, you squat with a heart so curled;
Carrying in your lap,
Degrees of scholars,
And taking a glimpse of the present day map;
To destroy a place with all your dollars;
And then call me a handicap;
NO, I am not;
For at least I don't cheat my fate;

Or live up to date;
Just to show;
Just to avow;
My pain so deep;
But tell me;
Oh! Tell me......
Is there someone who would really weep???

I read it aloud as a layer of optimism flew in me ...like cold water in the throat of the person who's thirsty for days...

Yeah, wisdom with a sprinkle of positive thoughts was all in me right now.

The World Was Indeed A Better Place To Live In. I Thought. Yeah, A Thought. A Thought That Wasn't There Earlier Perhaps. I Was An Optimist Now.....

The other morning I found lots of hearts near my bed......they carried a note from the king of hearts and Hearty that read....

"Congratulations! For an achievement, we all are celebrating here. And are proud of you and Gopsi. For the courage you have shown will be visiting you soon and this time you come here you got to stay longer with us."

"I promise to come soon and will stand on it just the way you did…"-Hearty

But How Can I Forget That Single Page That Inspired Me Way Back When I Came From The Hearts Planet…

I still have that one page, swinging, with the breeze, coming from the high in front of my eyes reading.

"I WISH, I ONLY WISH, IT WAS MY EARTH THAT I HAD BEEN TO…"

About the Author

Born in Srinagar , Kashmir valley Shilpa has seen the insanity of humans at a very early stage in her life. She was just three when her house was burnt down by terrorists, post that her family left the valley.

She says she indeed misses her mother land a lot . The inspiration to write comes from her motherland.

Shilpa has done her schooling from Dehradun and Jammu followed by perusing B.tech in IT from Chandigarh.

She has worked in 4 Punjabi feature films (regional cinema with brands like Eros and zee studios) as an actor.

She has worked in kids shows for Disney and big magic channel.

Writing and acting both are her food for life!

"The most beautiful thing about acting and writing both is that both come to me from the existence. When I act I forget my own existence and allow nothingness to rest in me, allowing the character I am playing to flow in my physical body. Acting is no less than meditation for me."

She also practices tarot card readings from past four years.

"I deeply realize the essence of all being connected: acting / writing and spirituality"
She quotes!

It's like when you don't aim for the fame , rather allow the existence to speak through you , you become an artist in your very being.

"When we act we are most of the time not being ourselves or doing the role what we really want to from within but when I write I am always happily doing what's storming in me to come out and flow through my ink."

Is what she quoted for "falling for love again " which was published in 2016.

Now she happily says " I only act and I only write when I know there is a calling and the universe wants to express through me , my ink, my expressions - the depth of my very being!"

Her family and brother is her strength for life. It's there unconditional love that germinates and fertilizes me.

www.ingramcontent.com/pod-product-compliance
Lightning Source LLC
Chambersburg PA
CBHW071416170626
46811CB00003B/1419